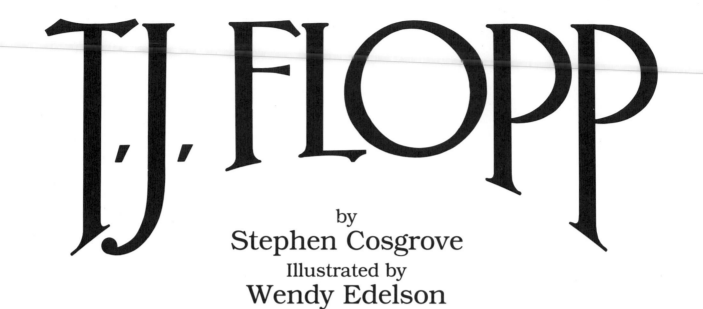

T.J. FLOPP

by
Stephen Cosgrove
Illustrated by
Wendy Edelson

MULTNOMAH

© 1989 by Stephen Cosgrove
Published by Multnomah Press
Portland, Oregon 97266
Printed in the United States.
All rights reserved.

Library of Congress Cataloging-in Publication

Cosgrove, Stephen.
    T.J.Flopp / by Stephen Cosgrove; illustrated by Wendy Edelson.
    p. cm.

    Summary: T.J. Flopp, a fearsome hunter, catches Miss Felicia Fuzzybottom who helps him acknowledge the tender emotions beneath his tough exterior.
    [1. Rabbits—Fiction.   2. Self-perception—Fiction.]
I. Edelson, Wendy, ill.   II. Title.
PZ7.C8187Tj   1989
[E]—dc20   89-9329
                                             CIP
                                             AC

ISBN 0-88070-281-8

89 90 91 92 93 94 95 96 97 - 10 9 8 7 6 5 4 3 2 1

To Eric Weber

Not a trapper, not a trader . . .
but the heart of a bunny all the same.

Stephen

arther than far and to the very edge of the horizon was a path bordered in lacy fern. If you walked down that path following the tracks of animals gone before, you would find a land called Barely There.

Tracks—little tracks, big tracks—wandered about all mixed together. The animals were there, you know, hiding with timid curiosity, watching as you walked down the paths.

If you followed those tracks a while, you would find a rustic trail that wound into the wild side of Barely There. There you would find creeks and streams of natural dreams where tanglebush draped graceful patterns into crystal mirrored waters. On the wild side it was said that not even the raccoons combed their hair when they got up in the morning.

It was a rough, natural beauty, and if you weren't careful your heart could get lost and you might never want to leave.

Deeper than deep in this wild jungle of pole pine and cedar the animals were a bit skittish. They were downright scared. For it was rumored that this land of wild nature's way was hunted and trapped by the greatest hunter and trapper in all of Barely There. If the truth be known, he was also the only trapper and hunter. For the creatures who lived there didn't feel a need to abuse nature. Everyone felt that way . . . everyone, that is, except the hunter himself.

Look about! There were signs that the hunter had indeed passed this way—a broken branch, a bootprint in the mud, and other not-so-subtle signs.

Beyond the pines and scratchy thickets, in a masculine mountain meadow, stood a crude cabin built of rough-sawn wood. The walls were chinked with musty moss, and a bent chimney pipe pointed a crooked, blackened finger at the sky as if to warn the clouds to stay away.

This was the home of the hunter—the roughest, toughest creature in all of Barely There.

As usual, when the sun set behind the purpled pines, the forest became strangely still. Birds didn't sing and chipmunks didn't chatter as something or someone crashed noisily through the forest. And there he was, the trapper of the woods, in all his ill-gotten glory.

He stood boldly at the edge of the clearing, his hat cocked back and a sneer twisted cross his face. With one hand on his hip and the other clutching an elephant gun, he seemed to dare anyone or anything to cross his path. This hunter was afraid of nothing, nothing at all. He could look at his own shadow on a scary night and just laugh, "Ha! Ha!"

This was one tough bunny . . . T. J. Flopp, trapper and trader.

COGNIGLIETTO

He stalked to his cabin and noisily stamped his feet on the sun-bleached wooden porch. With a mighty, furred hand he flung the door open and stomped inside.

The inside of the cabin was crude and horrible, for on the wall hung furs, the trophies of T. J.'s hunts gone by. Bunnies and bears, badgers and beavers—nothing in nature was safe or sacred from this hunter, this trapper.

He paid his trophies no mind, no courtesy, as he threw a bag of fresh trappings in the back room. Then he poured himself a cup of cold bitterroot tea, which he sloppily set down without a coaster or even a doily. He thumped into his chair and propped a muddy boot on the table.

SIGNOR TASSO

But nature is filled with twists and irony. For around his cabin, his cabin crude, grew the sweetest berries, the sweetest food in all the land of Barely There . . . the flutter-berries. But Flopp never so much as looked at the flutterberries, sweet on the vine, for he was so tough that he would rather eat thistles instead.

Squirrels and other rodents who hadn't heard the T. J. tales would boldly walk up to the cabin and take a berry or two. But they would have time to eat just one, for that was all the time it took for the trapper to leap into his slippers and grab his gun.

As the trespassing, berry-stained creature skittered away, T. J. would stand on his porch, shake his fist, and raise his rifle into the air.

"You had better git!" he would rumble and rail. "For if you don't git, you might end up a tiny trophy on my wall. Ha! Ha!" Then he would storm back inside and drink more cold bitterroot tea.

All would have stayed the same in this wild part of Barely There had not old Felicia Fuzzybottom, the school teacher who lived near Derby Downs, decided to can some preserves—some jellies and some jams. She had already made marmalade of honeysuckle vine, jam of lemon, jelly of lime, but there was just something missing.

"Harrumph," she muttered as she scratched her head. "I've cooked my preserves and in jars they are crammed, but what I don't have is any flutterberry jam. Hmm, the only flutterberries in the land grow near that old, run-down cabin of T. J. Flopp's. Well, he won't mind if I pick a basket or two."

So, just like that she threw her old knitted shawl across her shoulders and off she did hop to pick berries that belonged to T. J. Flopp.

Felicia picked and picked and had nearly filled her basket to the brim when old Flopp himself caught her red-handed, his gun in hand.

"Well, well, well," he crowed. "What do we have here? A berry poacher or a new trophy for my wall? Ha! Ha! Drop the basket and put up your hands. You have just been trapped by the greatest trapper in the land."

Old Miss Fuzzybottom was a bit nervous and more than a little bit scared; she was frightened nearly out of her wits. She dropped the basket as Flopp commanded and put her berry-stained hands high in the air. With that horrible gun stuck in her back, she marched up the rickety stairs, T. J. right behind.

"I don't know what I'm going to do with you. I could skin you and hang your hide on the walls like the others," he laughed maliciously. "I just don't know."

What a standoff—Felicia with her hands in the air, staring straight at the wall, afraid to look Flopp in the eye, and T. J., pacing about, making threats. As the hunter ranted and raved Felicia focused on the wall and began to look closely at the trophies. Suddenly, for some strange reason, she wasn't frightened anymore.

T. J. noticed her studying the wall and nervously said, "Okay, you've seen my trophies, now get out of here and warn the others to stay away. Tell them that T. J. Flopp is one tough cookie!" But old Miss Fuzzybottom didn't leave. "Maybe you didn't hear me," he said again. "I told you to git."

She ignored him completely as she walked about the room looking at all the furs nailed to the walls. The more she looked, the wider she smiled, and the more nervous Flopp became. He tried to get her to leave. He even offered to pick some berries for her, but old Felicia wouldn't budge.

For what hung on the walls weren't hides or trophies, but rather the fur of stuffed toys that had been abandoned. Miss Fuzzybottom walked about looking and laughing, and finally peeked in the back room. There were teddy bears, lions, and bunnies, and stuffed furry things that were terribly funny. She looked at old Flopp whose ears had drooped. "Why would you do this?" she asked in her gentle teacher's voice. "Why would you pretend you were something you were not?"

"Because," said Flopp with a big sigh, "everybody thinks bunnies are cute! When I was but a lad, the others laughed and called me cute. Why, they even called me fluffy! I didn't want to be cute anymore. I wanted to be rough, tough, and tumble."

"Ah, my dear T. J.," consoled Felicia as she patted his arm, "no matter how rough and tough your exterior, inside you will always be the same. For we are what we are."

Felicia Fuzzybottom taught old T. J. some marvelous things that day, and the next and the next. She taught him how to laugh at himself and not at others. She taught him how to cry from the heart and not worry about what others might be thinking. Most of all, she taught that grizzled old rabbit how to love himself for what he was, not for what he thought he should be.

As the story goes, Felicia Fuzzybottom and T. J. Flopp were married some months later in a bower of autumn leaves, surrounded by nature's gentle beauty.

On any cold winter's night you could find them cozied up together before a crackling fire where Felicia helped T. J. sew up the toys that later would be given to little girls and boys. She not only taught him to sew up the toys, but she helped him sew up his heart, which had needed mending for years.

Old Flopp even told Felicia what the initials T. J. stood for. For when T. J. was born, his momma and poppa named him what they felt in their hearts—Thoroughly Joyful. And that is what T. J., Felicia, and all the creatures were . . .

in the Land of Barely There.

Other books
in this series

Derby Downs
Fiddler
Gossamer
Ira Wordworthy
Shadow Chaser